BIONICLE®

Power Play

BIONICLE®

The legend comes alive in these exciting BIONICLE® books:

BIONICLE Chronicles
#1 Tale of the Toa
#2 Beware the Bohrok
#3 Makuta's Revenge
#4 Tales of the Masks

BIONICLE: Mask of Light
The Official Guide to BIONICLE
BIONICLE Collector's Sticker Book
BIONICLE: Metru Nui: City of Legends
BIONICLE: Rahi Beasts
BIONICLE: Dark Hunters

BIONICLE Adventures
#1 Mystery of Metru Nui
#2 Trial by Fire
#3 The Darkness Below
#4 Legends of Metru Nui
#5 Voyage of Fear

#6 Maze of Shadows
#7 Web of the Visorak
#8 Challenge of the Hordika
#9 Web of Shadows
#10 Time Trap

BIONICLE Legends
#1 Island of Doom

#2 Dark Destiny

BIONICLE®

Power Play

by Greg Farshtey

SCHOLASTIC INC.
New York Toronto London Auckland Sydney
Mexico City New Delhi Hong Kong Buenos Aires

For Michel and Marie,
with love

ISBN: 0-439-82804-X

12 11 10 9 8 7 6 5 4 3 2 1   6 7 8 9 10/0

Printed in the U.S.A.
First printing, August 2006

Characters

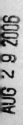

Island of Voya Nui

THE MATORAN

Garan	Onu-Matoran leader of the resistance
Balta	Ta-Matoran, able to improvise tools from anything lying around
Kazi	Ko-Matoran with many secrets
Velika	Po-Matoran inventor
Dalu	Ga-Matoran fighter
Piruk	Le-Matoran, skilled in stealth

THE PIRAKA

Zaktan	Green-armored Piraka
Hakvann	Crimson-armored Piraka
Reidak	Ebon-armored Piraka
Avak	Tan-armored Piraka
Thok	White-armored Piraka
Vezok	Blue-armored Piraka

ONE

For as far back as any Matoran villager could recall, the towering peak of Mount Valmai had looked down over Voya Nui. Despite the danger it represented — it was, after all, an extremely active volcano — the mountain was regarded as a guardian that would always be there.

In its time, Valmai had seen much. If the rock could have spoken, it would have told a tale of a thriving civilization, part of a mighty continent. Then the story would take a darker turn, as a portion of that continent was ripped away by a cataclysm and sent rocketing upward. The Turaga who lived there was killed in the ascent, along with many Matoran. When the new island finally came to rest in a strange sea, those villagers who had survived realized they had to fend for themselves or perish.

The battle for life had been fought every day. There were victories . . . and defeats, such as when a portion of land containing a large settlement mysteriously broke off and sank beneath the sea. To this day, the residents of Voya Nui still threw bundles of food and other objects into the water there as a means of commemorating those who had been lost.

The Matoran of Voya Nui had persevered for 1,000 years through storm, famine, drought, and even eruptions of Valmai. If there were others on the island, the Matoran did not know of them. They believed they were destined to be forever alone.

Valmai, of course, knew better.

Axonn sat down heavily on a slab of rock, sick at heart over what he had just witnessed. The wisdom of thousands of years lived inside him, power beyond almost any living being coursed through his muscles, and yet he could do nothing to save those who fought for right.

The six heroes called Toa Nuva and six brave Matoran had dared to challenge the evil Piraka who had seized control of the island. For a moment, it looked as if they might even win — the Piraka were in disarray and had been completely taken by surprise by the appearance of the Toa Nuva. But then, with one blow from the powerful Brutaka, all hope was lost.

Brutaka. How did it come to this?

He recalled when the two of them had first been dispatched to Voya Nui, long before the disaster that wrenched it free of its continent. They had been commanded by the secretive Order of Mata Nui to watch over the Matoran and, most importantly, the island itself. For the heart of the island concealed the most powerful Kanohi in existence — the Mask of Life.

Axonn and Brutaka had done their job well. When danger threatened the region, they dealt with it, all the while keeping their presence hidden from the Matoran. The first rule of the Order of Mata Nui was that its existence must never be revealed. Even the Toa, fellow guardians of light, were unaware of the Order's activities, or even that there was such an organization.

Some time after the cataclysm, Brutaka began to change. The Great Spirit Mata Nui had abandoned them, he insisted. He was dead, or perhaps had simply turned his back on the Matoran to pay attention to some other universe. Axonn argued that Mata Nui had simply been cast into a deep sleep but would someday awaken, and all would be made right again. Brutaka would not listen. He continued to carry out his duties, but his heart was no longer in his work.

Axonn knew his friend was on the edge. He simply did not realize how close Brutaka was to slipping into the darkness. . . .

Brutaka dumped the last of the unconscious Matoran onto the pile outside the Piraka stronghold. He had already taken care of the Toa Nuva — though still alive, barely, they were someplace where no one would ever find them. As for the Matoran, one was being interrogated and one had slipped away in the confusion following the battle. All the rest were destined for enslavement and hard labor on the slopes of Mount Valmai.

Axonn, Brutaka knew, would be horrified by what he had done. That was because his ex-partner was a fool, still sitting around waiting for the return of a Great Spirit who was long gone. The Piraka, and others like them, were the future — beings who took advantage of the chaotic state of the universe and seized power wherever they found it.

And the Kanohi mask they are searching for is the greatest power of all, he thought. *Too bad I am going to take it away from them. And for Axonn's sake, I hope he doesn't get in my way.*

He gave the Matoran one last look. They were still out. By the time they woke up, their fates would be sealed. Brutaka walked away.

Hissss . . .

The harsh sound made him turn back. A six-headed doom viper was slithering toward the fallen Matoran. The creature was known for its toxic breath, which was capable of killing any plant or animal exposed to it. One good exhale from it and all four Matoran would be history.

They will probably be better off, thought Brutaka. *All they have to look forward to is slaving for the Piraka, after all. . . .*

The doom viper inched closer. One of its heads watched Brutaka, ready to strike if he made a move. But he did not.

Closer. One of the Matoran began to stir. It was much too late for that.

The doom viper reared its heads back, ready to breathe its poison into the air. A short distance away, Brutaka's eyes narrowed.

A small vortex suddenly appeared in the air near the serpent. Before the doom viper could react, the vortex had grown larger. Powerful currents and eddies swirled around a heart of darkness. The poisonous Rahi tried to flee, but the vortex pursued, growing bigger with each moment. With an angry hiss, the doom viper was sucked inside and disappeared. A moment later, the vortex blinked out of existence.

Brutaka smiled. He had not had that much fun since he had used his Kanohi Mask of Dimensional Gates on a Tahtorak, dropping it into the center of Metru Nui just for fun. Of course, that had been long before Voya Nui and his crisis of belief . . . even then, the straight and narrow path had seemed a little too confining. Now that he was free of that life, he could use his mask to drop a doom viper into searing lava without thinking twice.

Still, the desire for amusement didn't explain why he had bothered to waste his energies saving Matoran who were doomed anyway. He hoped it didn't mean there was still some vestige of the old Brutaka in him. With a showdown with the Piraka looming, he could not afford any weakness.

He walked away, troubled. It was much easier to slay a powerful enemy, it seemed, than one's past.

Balta opened his eyes just the slightest bit and watched Brutaka depart. He had regained consciousness as the doom viper was closing in on him and his fellow Matoran. Had Brutaka not acted, he had no idea what he would have done. But there wasn't time to ponder the strange event.

The others were still unconscious. Dalu was missing, and so was Garan. Balta vaguely recalled hearing one of the Piraka say something about a "Chamber of Truth" to which the Matoran leader would be taken. It seemed unlikely he would ever be allowed to leave.

Balta started shaking the others awake, all the while trying hard not to think about what Garan might be going through at that moment.

Garan blinked at the sudden bright light coming through a slot in the stone wall. He had been sitting alone in a bare chamber for two hours, maybe more, waiting for something to happen. Now that the wait was over, he fought to keep his fear down.

"Simple questions, Matoran." The voice

coming through the slot belonged to Vezok, one of the most vicious of the Piraka. "Give honest answers, and you live."

"Yes. I know how much you Piraka admire honesty," Garan replied sarcastically.

"How many Matoran escaped us? How many are in your little resistance group?" asked Vezok.

"I haven't had time to count," said Garan. "We've been too busy planning your downfall."

The floor beneath Garan suddenly tilted. He almost lost his balance. A crack appeared between the left edge of the stone floor and the wall. A dim glow could be seen through the opening. It was accompanied by a searing blast of heat.

"You only get so many wrong answers, Matoran," said Vezok. "Then your time here is over and we bring in one of your friends. Someone will tell us what we want to know."

"You don't know Matoran very well," Garan said defiantly.

"Sure, I do," snorted Vezok. "Whining little

creeps always running to a Toa or a Turaga whenever anything goes wrong — that's what Matoran are."

"Did you see a Toa or Turaga here when you came to Voya Nui? We've faced everything this island could throw at us, alone, and we're still standing. And we'll still be standing when you and Zaktan and the rest are food for Takea sharks."

The floor tilted again, this time more violently. Garan fell. The crack had widened significantly and he could see molten lava through it. A few more such shifts in the floor and he would be dumped into the molten pool, never to be seen again.

"How much do you know about the Mask of Life?" growled Vezok.

Garan glanced at the lava. It wouldn't be a good way to end, but better than betraying his home and his friends. The Toa Nuva had told him enough about the mask so that he knew the Piraka must never have it.

"Nothing," Garan lied. "Why don't you tell me about it?"

Another sudden shift. Garan lost his footing again and actually slid a short distance toward the opening.

"Last chance," said Vezok. "A little while ago, I saw a lightning bolt shoot up into the sky and explode into six stars. Think carefully about your answer, Matoran — what was that? Another one of your tricks?"

Garan wasn't sure what to say. He had no idea what Vezok was talking about. He had a vague memory of a legend about stars suddenly appearing in the night sky, but that was connected to the coming of —

Toa? The word exploded in Garan's mind. *The Toa Nuva were defeated . . . but if those were spirit stars appearing in the sky, then it means six new Toa are on Voya Nui. No wonder Vezok sounds nervous. He wants to hear that we rigged the effect somehow . . . anything but that there are more Toa on his trail.*

Garan stood up again, knowing it might be for the last time. Then he smiled, a grin almost as broad as that of the Piraka but with none of the malice. "No, Vezok," he announced. "It was no trick of ours. I don't know who or where they are, but there are six new Toa on this island. And they are coming for you."

The floor jerked abruptly. Garan toppled over and began the long slide to his doom.

# TWO

My name is Kongu, he said to himself. *I come from the tree village of Le-Koro on the island of Mata Nui. If I lived someplace else before that time-era, I don't remember it.*

His companions stopped walking. He wondered if they were lost. It wasn't like there were many landmarks. None of them knew this strange island, anyway, which seemed so much less hospitable than Mata Nui. Heavy cloud cover made navigating by the stars impossible.

My name is Kongu, he repeated. *Back home, I was captain of the Gukko bird force, and an ever-skilled bird wrangler. When they told us we had to hurry-move to the city of Metru Nui, I helped build boats for the trip. But we didn't stay there long once we got there.*

The group was on the move again. Someone was pointing toward the volcano at the center of the island. That seems as good a place as any to start, he reasoned.

We went to Metru Nui because the Turaga-elders said we had to, in order to have any hope of quick-waking the Great Spirit, he continued. *But when we got there, we found out he wasn't just asleep — he was dying. Our heroes, the Toa Nuva, were sent to this island to seek-find something that would save him. When they didn't return, my friend Jaller persuaded a bunch of us to go deep-look for them.*

His thoughts trailed off. The rest of the story was too far-fetched to believe. Their masks had been stolen on the journey and replaced with others that were who knew how ancient. They had stumbled on canisters that transported them to the shores of Voya Nui. But before they could even get out and look around, something had happened.

What was it? Kongu wasn't sure. *There was a bright light-flash, and then a feeling that I was surrounded by a thousand Nui-Rama bugs, all buzzing at once. I quick-scrambled out of the canister and*

*there were Hahli, Jaller, Matoro, Nuparu, and Hewkii,
all looking like Toa. From the looks in their eyes, I
figured I must look like one, too.*

Somehow, though, he had never imagined
being a Toa would feel like this. Sure, he had raw
power in his muscles now and really awesome
armor. But it almost seemed like he had *too* much
energy and his mask just felt . . . weird.

"We're ever-wandering in the dark," he
said in as loud a voice as he could manage while
still whispering. "We have no idea where we are,
where the Toa-heroes are, or what else might be
on this island."

The others didn't look back. The only
sound was their metal-shod feet scraping against
the rocks.

"What's wrong with this carving?" Although
spoken in a whisper, Kongu's words were like a
shout.

"What do you want us to do?" asked Jaller.
"Turn back? Sit on the beach until morning and
talk everything out?"

"No," Kongu replied, trying to keep the

irritation out of his voice. "I just remember the Turaga's tales of what happens when Toa go off without a plan."

"He has a point," said Hahli.

Jaller stopped and turned around. Kongu expected him to keep arguing for moving on, but surprisingly he did not. "You're right, both of you. There was no point in listening to Turaga Vakama's tales if we aren't going to learn from them. But let's keep this short. The Toa Nuva may need us."

Toa Nuparu sat down on a rock. "I'll start by taking this Kanohi mask off for a second. I miss my old one. This one just doesn't feel —"

The area was suddenly lit up with a blinding glare. The other Toa shielded their eyes. Nuparu looked around to see what was causing the bright light, but the only thing he learned was that the illumination was everywhere he looked. What was going on?

"Put your mask back on!" snapped Hewkii.

Nuparu did as he was told, figuring the new Toa of Stone must have spotted some danger.

As soon as he had returned the Kanohi to his face, the light went out.

"That was strange," he said, his inventor's curiosity piqued.

"That was your face," answered Hewkii.

"Very funny," said Nuparu. "You're no vision of beauty yourself, Hewkii."

Hahli shook her head. "He's not joking. When you took your mask off, your face gave off a blinding glow. I couldn't even see your features."

Hewkii gestured toward a nearby cave. "Let's talk in there. No point in lighting up the night and letting everyone else here know our location."

The cave was dank and almost too small for all six of them to fit comfortably. Once inside, Hahli reached up and removed her mask. Her face, too, gave off an eye-searing radiance.

"Something's wrong," said Matoro. "I saw Toa Kopaka take his mask off once, and nothing like that happened. What kind of Toa are we?"

"I don't know," Hahli answered. It seemed very strange to hear her voice coming from inside the glow but not be able to see her mouth move. "But that's not the only unusual thing here. Take my mask. Tell me what you think."

Matoro reached out and took Hahli's Kanohi from her outstretched hand. He noticed immediately what she was talking about. Unlike any other mask he had ever handled, this one was pliable, less like armor and more like organic tissue. It felt warm to the touch. Suddenly, with a cry, he dropped it on the ground.

"It moved!" he yelled. "I mean . . . I think it moved . . . in my hand."

"Don't be ridiculous, masks can't move," said Hewkii, reaching out to recover the Kanohi. "They're objects, they're not —"

His fingers brushed against the mask. The Kanohi recoiled. Hewkii pulled back instantly. He looked up at the others and finished weakly, "Alive?"

"Put it back on, Hahli," said Jaller.

"I'm not so sure I want to," answered the Toa of Water. She gave a half-smile. "What if it bites?"

"Do it anyway," said Jaller. "I feel like I'm having a conversation with a lightstone."

Hesitantly, Hahli took her mask in hand. It never moved, tried to get away from her, or came across as anything but an inert object. She put it back on, cutting off the glare and allowing the others to lower their hands from their eyes.

"Well," said Nuparu. "I always wondered what it would be like to become a Toa. Somehow, I never pictured blinding features and moving masks. Think we can get a do-over?"

Jaller abruptly turned to Kongu. "What am I thinking?"

Before the Toa of Air could think of a response, he heard Jaller's voice in his head. It was saying something about a Rahi beast he had fought a long time back. Kongu "listened" for a few moments and then replied. "You're remembering a Muaka that threatened Ta-Koro three years ago. You and the Guard needed two days to drive-chase it off — and how did I know that?"

"It's a Mask of Telepathy, remember?" said

Jaller. "When we found it, Toa Takanuva was able to read Hahli's thoughts. It changed, like the Matoran masks we were wearing, into this more organic form, but it still works. Despite the masks' strange appearance, I am willing to bet they work the same as the ones we know . . . who knows, maybe better."

Nuparu stood up. "Great, but how do we use them? Remember how long it took the Toa Metru to master their mask powers in Turaga Vakama's tale? We have no training in using Great Masks and they won't activate just by our saying, 'I wish my mask worked.'"

No sooner were the words out of Nuparu's mouth then he shot straight up into the air and collided with the cavern roof. He fell back down, stunned.

"On the other hand, maybe they will," commented Hewkii.

Zaktan, leader of the Piraka, was not happy.

The operation on Voya Nui had seemed like it would be a simple one. Get on the island, snatch the Mask of Life from its hiding place, and get off — no mess, little risk, and great reward.

It had started to go wrong almost from the beginning. The Piraka had been unable to sustain the fraud that they were Toa here to help the local Matoran. A small group of the villagers rebelled, and time had to be wasted hunting them down. Then six Toa Nuva arrived on the island. They were also seeking the mask and it took a lengthy combat and the help of Brutaka to stop them.

And now there are more here....

None of the Piraka were talking openly about what they had seen, but that didn't mean they weren't reviewing the moment in their heads. Those six stars that appeared in the sky were spirit stars, Zaktan was sure of it, and each star was bound to a Toa. Apparently, this worthless little island on the south end of nowhere had suddenly become a gathering point for would-be heroes.

Add to that the fact that the Piraka themselves were turning on one another. Zaktan had already put down two open rebellions by his team. There were bound to be more. Eventually, he might have to kill one of the other five just to make a point.

It would be worth it. Nothing mattered more than getting his hands on the Mask of Life. Let the Matoran burn in the lava, let the others on his team fall to Toa, and let the rest of Voya Nui sink into the sea — as long as he had that mask.

The others didn't understand. They thought it was just one more Kanohi. Zaktan knew it was more, although he couldn't put his finger on just how he knew. But each time he closed his eyes to rest, he awoke more certain than ever that the mask was the key to ultimate power.

Legend stated that the Mask of Life was forged by the Great Beings long before the coming of Mata Nui or the creation of the city of Metru Nui. It was no exaggeration to say that the life or death of the universe was tied to that mask. Under normal circumstances, it might be donned once every 5,000 years by a Toa whose destiny called for such a sacrifice. For the wearer of that Kanohi, it was said, would burn with the energies it unleashed.

These, of course, were not normal circumstances. The Great Spirit Mata Nui was comatose and had been so for 1,000 years. Metru Nui had been abandoned by the Matoran, then reclaimed. Entire cities had been destroyed or else torn from their home continents, as Voya Nui had been. Visorak had run wild. Rahi were still on the rampage in some areas. The Brotherhood of Makuta was at war with the Dark Hunters, and both sides eliminated any Toa they ran across. Chaos ruled.

That explains why the Toa are here, and why they want the mask. They think they can restore order with it, the fools, Zaktan thought. *Order is dead and buried. The universe belongs to anyone strong enough to seize the stars and crush them in his grasp.*

The emerald-armored Piraka was reluctant to admit even to himself that he didn't really know exactly what the mask could do. He privately doubted that any one Kanohi could slay a universe. The legends were probably just that, *legends* — comforting little lies passed down by weak-minded Matoran. They were designed to convince the Matoran that all would be well in the end, and that there was nothing truly scary lurking in the darkness.

Zaktan smiled. *It is obvious the tale-tellers never met a Piraka.*

Hakann woke up. His head felt like a Kikanalo had been dancing on it. He coughed up some rock dust and decided it was time to try getting up.

Shoving aside some rubble, he stood up. He was in the Piraka stronghold, where Zaktan had left him. Foolishly, Hakann had calculated the Piraka leader might be ripe for overthrow, and he acted on his own rather than allying with others. Zaktan had beaten him with embarrassing ease and then, in a show of complete disrespect, had allowed the rebellious Piraka to live.

Hakann took a deep breath and tried to calm himself. Acting from emotion was what had gotten him defeated. He had to be smart. He had to have a plan. Most importantly, he had to get someone else to take the risks next time.

Conveniently, three other Piraka — Avak, Reidak, and Thok — chose that moment to enter the chamber. Hakann purposely slumped against the wall, trying to look more badly injured than he really was. When they asked him what had happened, he would tell them Zaktan attacked for no reason, and convince them they would be next.

That's what he *would* have done, anyway. But the three walked right past him with barely a glance, as if a wounded Hakann was something they saw every day — or wished they did.

"I should throw you off cliffs more often," Reidak said to Thok. "It's fun."

The white-armored Piraka simply glared. Avak stepped in between them, snarling, "Shut up and listen! Brutaka beat six Toa Nuva with one swing of his blade. What happens if he comes after us?"

"I point him at Reidak and get out of the way," Thok replied.

"He got in a lucky shot," Reidak said. "Took the Toa by surprise. I could have handled him."

"Like the way you handled Zaktan?" Thok growled. "We had him caged and you freed him, you idiot!"

"Enough!" Hakann shouted. The others turned to look at him, then resumed walking. But the crimson-armored Piraka was not going to be denied. "You're missing the obvious," he continued. "I expect that from Reidak, but you, Thok. Where is that cunning brain you are always bragging about? Has it rotted from the heat of Voya Nui's lava flows?"

"Shut up, Hakann," said Thok.

"All right," Hakann replied. "Then I guess you don't want to know that Zaktan was conspiring with Brutaka long before you knew he existed. The two of them have a pact, and who else wants to bet it involves five dead Piraka and Zaktan with the Mask of Life?"

The other three stopped in their tracks. Ordinarily, they wouldn't believe much of anything that came from Hakann's grinning mouth.

But they also knew what Zaktan was capable of, and if he had a being like Brutaka at his side . . .

"Forget this," said Avak. "Let's get off this rock. I'd rather take my chances with the Dark Hunters than get snapped in two by Zaktan and his pet monster."

"I hate to risk leaving Zaktan in control of the Mask of Life — if it exists," said Thok. "But unless we can split Brutaka away from him —"

"Are you finished?" Hakann said, sounding bored. "There will be no splitting. There will be no snapping. Instead, you will listen to me and do exactly what I say . . . assuming, of course, you want to live to see another rainy day on Voya Nui."

Hakann waited a moment for his words to sink in, and then smiled. "We can handle Zaktan. Brutaka is the real threat. So we get him before he gets us, and here's how we do it."

The other three Piraka listened carefully to the words that followed. By the time Hakann was finished, they were smiling, too.

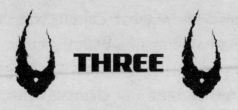 **THREE**

Garan was about to die.

He could feel the intense heat of the lava and his hands losing their grip on the smooth stone of the floor. He realized with surprising calm that the dark gray rock and the fingers of his left hand might well be the last things he ever saw in this life. In his last moments, he voiced a hope that Balta would take over for him as leader and drive the Piraka from Voya Nui's shores.

His head hurt. At first, he thought it was caused by the proximity of the molten inferno that waited for him. Then he realized it was a sound that was piercing his brain, barely audible yet potent nonetheless. He had heard that sound before. *What was it?*

The sound increased in volume. He wondered if this was some final torture of Vezok's before the end.

Now the mind-shredding vibration was replaced by a different sound, that of a stone wall shattering into rubble. Rock and dust rained down on Garan. He looked over his shoulder to see one wall of the Chamber of Truth gone and four Matoran standing there.

Balta got a running start and made a successful leap over the gap in the floor. As he started to help Garan up, the Onu-Matoran spotted Vezok coming up behind the others. Giving a yell, Garan fired his pulse bolts, striking the Piraka square in the chest and sending him flying.

Balta and Garan leapt toward safety, just barely catching a handhold on the rock. Piruk, Kazi and Velika scrambled to help them up. Vezok had already recovered from Garan's initial attack and was heading back toward the group.

The Piraka charged, his massive arm coming down to deliver a blow to Piruk. Balta shot between him and his target and raised his twin repellers. Vezok's fist met the weapons and he was immediately flung back, struck down by his own power.

"Go! Run!" yelled Balta. All five Matoran broke for the foothills. By the time Vezok's senses returned, they were gone.

Once they were sure they were not being pursued, the members of the Matoran resistance stopped and caught their breath. Garan looked around and noticed not all were present. "Where's Dalu?"

"I don't know," Balta replied. "She wasn't there when I woke up. Maybe she escaped before they brought us to the Chamber of Truth."

"We need to find her," said Garan. "And we need to find the Toa."

Piruk shook his head. "The Toa Nuva are almost certainly dead. The Piraka would not leave them alive. It's hopeless."

Velika smiled. "There once was a Matoran who was stricken with thirst. He left his shelter to seek out his water bucket, but when he found it, it was dry. Puzzled, he lifted it up and discovered a hole in the bottom had let the water leak out. Angry that his thirst could not now be quenched, he cursed the bucket, cursed the island, and cursed his need for water. So frustrated was he that he never noticed water had begun to fall from the sky."

There was a long silence. Finally, Kazi sank his head into his hands and said, "I know I am going to regret asking this . . . but what does that mean?"

"It means don't get so caught up in looking for salvation from one direction that you miss seeing it coming from another," said Garan. "The Toa Nuva may be captured, or they may be dead. But six new stars appeared in the sky — and six new Toa walk this island."

"What makes you think they will fight any better than the Toa Nuva did?" asked Piruk.

Garan recalled the image of the six Toa Nuva, battered into unconsciousness by Brutaka. It had been the last thing he had seen before darkness claimed him as well. "All I know, Piruk, is their fate cannot be any worse."

Nuparu wasn't sure whether to shout with joy or scream with terror.

Just after he and the other new Toa had left the cave, an idle thought crossed his mind about his Kanohi mask. A second later, he was flying high above the rocky ground, swooping and diving like a manic Gukko bird. For someone who had spent virtually his whole life laboring in underground tunnels, it was exhilarating and hor-rifying at the same time.

Down below, the other Toa watched him, eyes wide with shock. Behind his mask, Kongu could not keep the resentment off his face. After all, he was the best Gukko rider on Mata Nui — if anyone got a Mask of Flight, it should have been him.

"What's he doing up there?" asked Hahli.

The answer came to Kongu almost imme-diately. "He doesn't know how to safe-land." There was more, but he chose not to share it. Ever since he had triggered his mask power for Jaller, he had been unable to turn it off. His mind was now full of the babble of everyone else's thoughts. Jaller was worried they had plunged into more than they could handle; Hahli was struggling to remember all that Toa Nuva Gali had taught her; and Hewkii was a little upset no one had commented on the fact that his armor had turned from brown to yellow when he became a Toa.

Nuparu banked at the last moment and just avoided smashing into a peak. Convinced someone had to do something before they wound up short one Toa, Jaller turned to Matoro. "Can you use your ice power to, I don't know, hold him in place for a second and —"

The Toa of Fire stopped abruptly. Matoro was lying on the ground, completely still, as if he had just been struck dead. Jaller, along with the others, rushed to his side. Nuparu's plight was now forgotten.

"Matoro? Matoro!"

"Is he —?" Hewkii asked quietly.

"I don't know," said Jaller. "I don't think so. What could have happened? We were standing right beside him. No one could have attacked."

"Perhaps it's these masks," answered Hewkii. "Maybe they're trying to kill us."

"No, I don't understand it either," said Hahli. Jaller looked up to see that she was facing away from Matoro, apparently having a conversation with empty air. He wondered for a moment if Hahli had gone crazy.

"Just relax," Hahli continued. "We'll figure this out, I promise."

"Figure what out?" said Hewkii. "Who are you talking to?"

"Well, she *thinks* she's happy-talking to Matoro," reported Kongu. "Which is obviously ridiculous, since Matoro is over here and isn't much of a conversationalist right now."

"You're wrong," said Hahli. "Only his body is over there. His spirit is floating in the air over here, and no, I don't know how it happened. Matoro thinks it has something to do with his mask. He says there are five Matoran not far away who are looking for us."

"How does he know?" asked Jaller, rapidly running out of patience with this increasingly bizarre situation.

Hahli glanced down at the ground before answering, clearly realizing the others were about to think she had lost her mind. "Um, well, he says he flew through the mountains ... straight through the rock, like it wasn't there ... and he saw them ... but they couldn't hear him or see him."

Hewkii, Jaller, and Kongu looked at one another, then looked at her. Finally, Kongu muttered in disgust, "Sure. He's flying, Nuparu's flying, everyone's flying but the one who knows *how* to fly."

Jaller frowned. "Can he reverse ... whatever happened?"

Hahli turned away from the others and said, "Try."

On the ground, Matoro suddenly stirred. The light in his eyes flared to life. He jerked awake like someone emerging from a very bad dream. "What? Where? Mata Nui, what a dream. . . ."

Hahli knelt down beside him. "I don't think

it was a dream. I saw you, even if the others didn't."
She smiled. "And that's some power you have."

"I'm not sure I want to know what my mask
does," Hewkii remarked. "It might turn me into
a Le-Matoran or something."

"You wish," Kongu shot back, managing
a grin.

Jaller ignored them, focusing on Matoro.
"Which way are these Matoran? Keep in mind,
we can't walk through solid rock."

Matoro pointed to the north. "They're
scared, Jaller, of something or someone called
'Piraka.' I got the feeling they are the only Matoran
on the island still free."

Jaller helped the new Toa of Ice to his feet.
"Let's go find them. The more I find out about
this place, the more worried about the Toa Nuva
I become."

There was no direct route to the spot where
Matoro had sighted the Matoran, just a winding
path through the foothills and into the mountains. At one point, Hahli suggested that Matoro

use his mask power again to find them, but the Toa of Ice refused, still disturbed from his last experience. Jaller finally coaxed Nuparu close enough to the ground to communicate what they were looking for and asked him to scout from the air.

He returned within a few minutes to say he had not seen any Matoran, but that he had spotted something that was most definitely not a villager or a Toa. "A face only a mother Manas could love," Nuparu said. "And he's armed."

"Only one?" asked Jaller.

Nuparu nodded. "Blue armor, nasty spikes, weapons in both hands. I saw him make a rock explode just by glancing at it."

"Sounds like someone we should talk to."

"Yeah, let's take him down," agreed Hewkii. When the others turned to look at him, he smiled and said, "Hey, I'm Toa of Stone now. A rock has been destroyed — I have to avenge it, don't I?"

Vezok's eyes were riveted on the dark sky. He could have sworn he had seen a flying figure a few moments before. Whatever it was had spotted him, then turned tail and soared off. Worse, it didn't look like just some flying Rahi.

The last time he had seen someone "fly" on this island, it had been Reidak and he had been hurled into the air by —

Suddenly, he knew just what he had seen. For an instant, he considered running back and getting the others. Then the potential for the kind of victory that vaulted one to leadership crossed his mind, not to mention all the loot that might be his. *The other Piraka,* he decided, *would really just get in the way.*

He broke into a run, already anticipating the battle to come.

FOUR

The journey of the new Toa came to an abrupt halt.

They had arrived at the edge of a vast gorge. Below, a stream of molten lava wound its way through the rock. The gap was too wide to jump and too long to go around without hours of walking. But the Matoran that Toa Nuparu had spotted were somewhere on the other side. They might not have hours to spare to reach them.

Jaller turned to Nuparu. "You'll have to fly us over."

"Now wait a minute," Kongu broke in. "Let's be sensible. Nuparu and I can switch masks, and I'll do the flying."

Jaller was going to respond, but never got the chance. Instead, it was Nuparu who spoke up. "That does make sense. I can't argue with it.

But destiny, for whatever reason, gave me this mask. There has to be a reason for that."

"Destiny has a sense of humor?" jeered Kongu.

"I think I am supposed to have it. I'm not going to give it up, not yet," Nuparu replied. Then he broke into a grin. "Besides, flying's kind of fun."

"Wonderful," said Kongu, shaking his head. "They can deep-carve that on our memorial stones —'But at least Nuparu had fun.'"

Nuparu rose into the air and grabbed onto Kongu. Before the Toa of Air could protest, Nuparu had him halfway across the gorge. When they reached the other side, he unceremoniously dropped Kongu to the ground.

"This is amazing," cried Nuparu. "Why, if I built some tools that would help me stay level and steer, this mask would work even better."

In short order Hewkii and Matoro crossed over in similar fashion. Hahli had wanted to go last — she had a terrible headache that seemed to get worse the closer they got to the center of the island — but Jaller insisted that he should act as rear guard. Nuparu picked her up gently and started across.

This time, the passage was not so smooth. A fierce wind kicked up when he was partway across. Inexperienced at flying, Nuparu did not know how to compensate. Thrown off balance, he lost his grip on Hahli.

Jaller watched in horror. No doubt any of the Toa could save her with their elemental powers, but they had had little to no practice using them so far. A miscalculation would mean her death.

Later, Jaller would realize he never actually gave any thought to what he did. Instead, he just ran, leapt out into midair, and caught Hahli. The added weight should have sent them both plunging into the lava, but instead Jaller used the change in momentum to execute a perfect midair somersault that carried them toward the far edge. He landed feetfirst on the lip of the gorge. The other Toa just stared at him in disbelief.

"Whoa," said Hewkii. "That was a new one."

"Even Toa Lewa would have admired that move," added Kongu. "Who taught you that?"

Jaller put Hahli down and shrugged. "No one. It was the only thing to do, but . . . it shouldn't have worked. We should both be in the lava. I can't understand how . . ."

"Could it be your mask?" asked Hahli.

Kongu chuckled. "What, it's a Mask of Leaping?"

Nuparu landed next to the group. "Or something much more powerful," he said. "We should test it, Jaller. And . . . I'm sorry about what happened."

All of the Toa waited for Kongu to make some cutting remark. Instead, the Toa of Air threw his arm around the shoulders of the Toa of Earth and said, "Come here, Toa-hero. Let me quick-teach you a little something about updrafts and downdrafts. I don't want you crashing and breaking that mask."

Hidden among the rocks, Vezok watched the six newcomers. They were Toa, all right, but novices. This, he decided, would be no trouble at all. He chewed up and spit out rookie Toa. In fact, it might even be fun to use zamor spheres on a few of them and let them fight one another.

Smiling, he emerged from his hiding place and took aim.

Matoro spotted the threat too late. Even as he shouted out a warning, Vezok's zamor sphere struck his body. There was a flash of electricity as it passed through him.

The Toa waited. Vezok waited. Most of all, Matoro waited to see what would happen.

Nothing.

Vezok looked at his launcher, annoyed. He fired again. Same result. "What's going on here?" he grumbled. "You should be enslaved."

"Oh, is that what that does?" said Matoro. He raised his ice sword. "Then I don't feel so bad about doing this."

Matoro expected a blast of ice to fly from the blade, much like he had seen Kopaka Nuva

43

create a hundred times. But this was different. His blade glowed with a bright light, and the blue-white beam of ice that it hurled was interlaced with lightning. It struck Vezok dead on, simultaneously freezing and jolting him.

The blue-armored Piraka hit the ground hard. The force of the attack had been unexpected, but he wasn't worried. He could already feel this new Toa's power being added to his own. Laughing, he launched a blast of electrically charged ice at the red-and-yellow Toa nearby.

This time, Jaller knew it was the mask. There was no possible way he could dodge the ice, yet somehow he managed to twist his body out of the way. For a moment, he almost sensed that the mask was regarding him with approval.

"You picked the wrong Toa to throw snowballs at," he snapped. His weapon, too, was glowing, and the flames it shot sizzled with pure electricity. Again, Vezok was struck, and again he went down. But he didn't stay down.

"Get ready," said Matoro. "He duplicated my power when I used it on him. He'll do the same with Jaller's, but I'm guessing he can't handle more than one power at a time."

Vezok raised both arms and smiled broadly. "Guess again."

Blasts of fire and ice flew from the Piraka's hands. Matoro and Hahli were sent reeling by the unleashed elemental energy. *That's two down,* Vezok thought. *There should be a quick way to take out the other four, but . . .*

He frowned. Ever since the accident, he had lost the ability to think tactically the way he used to. He was still smarter than he looked, but that intellectual edge was missing. Still, he knew who had stolen it from him, and he would get it back as soon as these Toa were dead.

Hewkii, Kongu, Jaller, and Nuparu stood shoulder to shoulder. The Toa of Air reached out with his Mask of Telepathy to probe the Piraka, but recoiled almost immediately. "Muaka bones, it's a pesthole in there," he exclaimed.

"I've crawled through Nui-Rama nests that were cleaner."

"Who are you? What do you want here?" asked Jaller.

"The name is Vezok," answered the Piraka. My partners and I already claimed this island by right of conquest. And we don't like trespassers."

"That's too bad," said Nuparu. "We're —"

"I know what you are," Vezok cut him off. "Toa. I could smell you a kio away. You all have that 'doomed do-gooder' stench."

Hewkii hefted a huge boulder. Vezok only smiled. "Drop that or I freeze-fry your two pals," he said.

The Toa of Stone shrugged and casually tossed the rock aside. Only Matoro noticed it hit another rock, ricochet, hit a second, and so on.

"Do yourselves a favor," Vezok continued. "Clear off Voya Nui while you still can, or you'll wind up like those other Toa. You can't beat one Piraka, let alone six."

Now it was Hewkii's turn to smile. "Guess again."

The boulder ricocheted one last time and slammed into Vezok's back. Stunned more by the surprise of the blow than from its force, Vezok stumbled forward. Nuparu triggered his mask power and shot through the air, slamming into the Piraka's midsection and knocking him to the ground. The other three Toa closed in.

Vezok snarled, energies crackling around his open palms. Jaller rested the tip of his energized flame-sword on the Piraka's throat. "Think about it," said the Toa of Fire. "Can you get off a blast before I do? Are you fast enough?"

Jaller cocked his head and locked eyes with Vezok. "I don't need a Mask of Telepathy to know what's going through your head. You figure we're new to being Toa, maybe not quick enough or skilled enough to use our powers. And you're right. But, see, there's only one problem — I'm so new I can't always control my flame. I might want to just singe you, Vezok . . . but poor, novice Toa that I am, I could slip . . . and burn your head clean off."

Vezok lowered his hands. Kongu turned

away to check on Matoro and Hahli. His mask power was almost impossible to turn off and the last thing he wanted was any more exposure to Vezok's thoughts.

"Get up," ordered Jaller. "You're going to take us to those other Toa you mentioned."

"Sure," Vezok replied. "I've never liked the smell of something burning . . . especially when it's me."

Jaller shoved the Piraka ahead of them. Hewkii and Matoro took the flanks, with Kongu acting as rear guard. They had gone only a short distance when the Toa of Air picked up a disturbing image from Vezok's mind. He cried out, but not fast enough. The Piraka had hurled an ice blast and a fire blast at each other, creating a wall of steam when they met. Kongu used his control over wind to dissipate the cloud, but by that time, the Piraka was gone.

"Do we track him?" asked Matoro.

Jaller shook his head. "He knows the island. We don't. But he may be our only lead to the Toa Nuva."

Power Play

An Onu-Matoran stepped out from behind a cluster of rocks. "If you follow him, he will pick you off one by one. He will be heading back to the stronghold to warn Zaktan of your approach. We need to make our plans before he reaches there."

"Zaktan? Stronghold? Who are you?" asked Matoro, feeling like he had walked in on one of Hahli's tales in the middle.

"My name is Garan. I will tell you my story on our journey. I'd suggest you listen, if you ever hope to leave this island alive."

Garan led the Toa on a long journey, sticking close to the coastline all the way. He explained that the waters around Voya Nui were so treacherous that the Piraka did not expect enemies to arrive by sea. They focused their attention on the air. Apparently, they expected someone to come looking for them, someone infinitely more frightening than Toa.

"You are Toa, aren't you?" he asked at one point. "But you don't look like Toa Nuva."

"We're not," said Jaller. He thought about the lightning bolts that had unleashed their powers, the glow of their faces behind their masks, the way their weapons radiated energy. Then he said, "No, not Toa Nuva. Toa Inika."

The name caught the other Toa by surprise, but it made sense — *inika* was the Matoran word for "the energies of a star." No one reacted quite as much as Hahli, though. For a brief moment, the headache she felt intensified, and then it lessened almost completely. She allowed herself a moment of relief before wondering just what had changed. Was it the name Jaller had thought up, or was it the sight of the volcano in the distance that had caused the pressure on her mind to ease . . . or was it both? Almost as if in response, she felt a small jolt of pain.

Her hands flew up to her mask. As soon as she took it off, all the pain stopped.

So it is the Kanohi, she said to herself. *Yet it's not an attack, somehow I know that. No, the mask is trying to direct us. But where?*

"This way," said Garan. He led the Toa

Inika through a tunnel in the rock. It wound up and up, growing narrower as it rose. At the top, Garan slid aside a stone and disappeared inside a hole.

Jaller led the Toa through the opening. Inside was a small chamber. Garan and four other Matoran waited within.

"This is all of you?" asked Kongu. "Five Matoran on an entire island?"

"Five still free," Balta answered.

"Make that six."

The two groups turned to see Dalu slipping in through another entrance. She spared a smile for Balta before giving her report to Garan. "I tried to get away but didn't make it very far. I saw enough to know you're right. The Piraka alliance is fracturing."

"Then it is time to strike," said Kazi.

"Never a better one," Dalu agreed. "Hakann, Reidak, Avak, and Thok are nowhere to be found. Zaktan is in a rage over it. No one is watching the Matoran workers on the slopes of the volcano."

"Slow down," said Matoro. "What's going on here? Where are the Toa Nuva?"

"Dead, if they're lucky," Garan replied. "If they're not, Zaktan has them. They are looking for a treasure hidden on this island — your friends said it was a mask needed to save the life of the Great Spirit. They enslaved our people to help them get their claws on it. We are going to stop them."

Garan walked up to Jaller and looked up at the Toa of Fire. "Your fellow Toa tried to help and paid the price. If you want to turn and go, we will understand. But if you want to aid us, you must decide now. This chance to hit the Piraka hard may not come again."

Jaller instantly knew what his decision would be, but he was determined not to be Tahu or Vakama or other Toa who had acted rashly. He turned to the others. One by one, they nodded their heads. Then he looked back at Garan.

"You point us in the right direction," said the Toa of Fire. "We'll handle the hitting."

 **FIVE**

Jaller hefted the launcher in his left hand, appreciating the lightweight feel and the efficiency of design. Velika had handed them out to all the Toa Inika before they departed the Matoran refuge. He had made some comment about flames being the surest way to stop a fire, which made no sense to Jaller at all.

The Toa and Matoran resisters had split into three teams. Jaller, Hahli, Dalu, and Piruk were headed for the northern face of the volcano. Velika had assured them that the ammunition in the launchers would be able to free the enslaved Matoran workers.

"What are these things loaded with?" Jaller asked as they walked.

"Keep quiet and keep moving," Dalu replied. Hahli's eyes widened at her tone.

"Don't mind her," Piruk said quietly. "She's

just edgy. Anyway, that building we were in is an old fortress built long before Voya Nui floated where it is now. We were securing underground entrances to it when Velika found this silvery pool. None of us knew what it was, but he insists it will free our friends from the effects of the zamor spheres. I snuck into the Piraka stronghold, stole some spheres, and Velika filled them up with the stuff. Who knows if they'll work . . . but even death would be better than being slaves to the Piraka, I guess."

"Maybe you two would like to take a rest and discuss the history of Voya Nui?" Dalu snapped. "I'm sure Toa Hahli and I can manage this mission without you."

"Dalu!" Hahli exclaimed. "We're all on the same team here. Let's not fight among ourselves. In Metru Nui —"

"Right," said Dalu. "I'm sure where you come from, Ga-Matoran are all gentle peacemakers who never raise their voices. That's what they . . . we . . . were like where I came from too. But I have news for you, sister — this isn't Metru

Nui. We don't have time to be polite. It's fight, or end up like them."

Dalu was pointing up at the slope of Mount Valmai. A small group of Matoran were digging into the side of the volcano, moving slowly and mechanically. An unhealthy glow radiated from their eyes.

The Ga-Matoran crouched down. "We're in luck. No Piraka around. But if any of the workers spot us, they'll shout out an alarm and we'll have a fight on our hands. So aim true."

"You expect us to launch these spheres at them?" Hahli asked in disbelief. "When we don't know what effects they might have?"

"Well, we could go ask them nicely to stop being worker drones for the Piraka, but somehow I don't think that will work," Dalu replied acidly. "If Velika says we use these things, then we use them."

"She's right," said Jaller, already taking aim. "Maybe it's not what the Toa Nuva or the Turaga would do, but they're not here . . . and like she said, this isn't Metru Nui."

Jaller triggered the launcher. The sphere flew straight and true, striking one of the Matoran in the chest and passing harmlessly through his body. For a few moments, nothing happened. Then the sickly glow faded and the Matoran looked around as if he had just awakened from a long sleep.

The other Matoran workers noticed immediately that something was not right. They picked up their tools and started toward the now-freed member of their group.

Hahli recalled a tale she had once heard. Toa Nokama had been very ill and she'd had to consume an herb to be healed. These spheres, she decided, were like that herb — the only hope for a cure. With that in mind, she started using her launcher.

She was no Hewkii when it came to aim, but she had not been a kolhii champion without learning something about accuracy. Between them, she and Jaller managed to hit and heal each of the Matoran before the alarm could be raised.

Dalu rushed out to greet her friends. "Piruk will take you to a place of safety, but you have to move fast," she said to the confused Matoran. "He'll explain what's been happening on the way. Once you have rested, you'll have your chance to fight. Understand?"

The villagers nodded and followed the Le-Matoran down the slope. Dalu turned to Jaller and Hahli, saying, "Next time, launch faster." Then she resumed walking, saying quietly over her shoulder, "And thanks."

"Tell me again where we're going," said Toa Matoro. He, Toa Hewkii, Balta, and Kazi had been hiking for what felt like days, and they were still only halfway up the mountain pass.

"Just trust me," Kazi replied.

Matoro glanced at Hewkii, and both clenched their Toa weapons a little bit tighter. After all, the Toa Nuva had come here and obviously something bad had happened to them. Who was to say they weren't betrayed by the very beings they were trying to help?

"You said you have an ally up here," said Toa Hewkii. "If he's so powerful and on your side, where has he been all this time? Why did he let the Piraka take over the island?"

Kazi started to say something, then stopped. It was Balta who answered, saying, "Sometimes you can't do what your heart tells you to . . . sometimes you have a duty to something greater than yourself."

The Ta-Matoran stopped and turned to look at the Toa. "This is important. In the battle to come, Matoran may die, Toa may die, and it doesn't matter. None of it matters. The only thing that counts is keeping the Mask of Life out of the hands of the Piraka. If we all have to die and this island has to be blown to fragments to stop them, then that's what we'll do."

Hewkii shook his head. "There has to be a better way than total destruction. What kind of a victory is that?"

Balta resumed his quick pace up the pass. "If you wanted nice, clean victories, Toa, you should have stayed on this Metru Nui you came from."

Kazi suddenly darted off the path to the right and scrambled over the rocks. *This is it,* thought Hewkii. *He disappears, and the trap is sprung.*

But there was no sudden ambush. Instead, the rocks slid aside, as if moved by a giant hand, to reveal a cavern mouth. A light glowed from somewhere far within. Kazi leaped back down to stand beside the others.

"He's in there," said the Ko-Matoran.

"Who?"

"Axonn," Kazi and Balta said simultaneously. Then the two looked at each other, startled.

"I thought I was the only one who knew —" said Kazi.

"I met him not long ago. He saved my life," said Balta. "How long have you known he was here? Why didn't you tell anyone?"

"I think we should save the questions," Hewkii said, pointing into the cave.

An armored figure had staggered into view. His size and power were unmistakable, yet he could barely stay on his feet and the axe he dragged behind him seemed too much to carry. When he saw Kazi, he reached out a hand. Then he began to fall.

Toa Matoro acted quickly, using his ice power to create a soft bed of snow for the stranger to land on. Then the four of them rushed to Axonn's side. His armor was battered and scorched, and some of the muscle tissue inside had been damaged as well. For a moment, Matoro wondered if they were in time only to watch him die.

"Kazi . . . ," Axonn said weakly. "You and these Toa . . . you have to hurry. . . ."

"What is it?" said the Ko-Matoran. "Who did this to you?"

"Brutaka," the wounded figure replied. "Said he was going to tell the Piraka how to find the Mask of Life . . . then steal it from them. He doesn't understand . . . what might happen . . . I tried to stop him, but . . ."

"Where was he headed?" asked Balta.

"The stronghold," said Axonn. "I thought I could bring him back to the way of Mata Nui . . .

but he is lost in the darkness. Stop him . . . stop him even if you have to kill him to do it."

The light in Axonn's eyes winked out then. Kazi knelt beside him and said, "He's alive, just unconscious. I should stay and —"

"No. We need you," said Balta. He looked up at Hewkii and Matoro. "And we need you, too. Brutaka is the one who beat your friends — maybe killed them — we don't know. If he gets his hands on the Mask of Life, or the Piraka do, the universe dies screaming."

Hewkii looked into the eyes of Balta. It was impossible to read their expression, cloaked in darkness as they were, but Hewkii knew they must contain the same steely resolve as Tahu Nuva's orbs. He wondered for a split second how destiny chose who would be a Toa and who wouldn't, for surely this Ta-Matoran had the heart of a hero.

"We'll pick up the others on the way," said the Toa of Stone. "And then I'll show Brutaka how a kolhii ball feels when it's kicked into orbit."

* * *

Garan ducked as a concussive blast shattered a nearby boulder.

"It's getting our range," he said. "We need to withdraw."

Toa Kongu dove and rolled across the rocky ground, blasts sizzling the air just above him. When he was behind cover again, he turned to Garan and Velika. "And do what? Come back later when it's deep-asleep? It's a machine!"

Garan peered around the rock. The nektann, robotic guardian of the Piraka stronghold, spotted him instantly and fired. Garan barely got out of the way in time. "I'm only suggesting that maybe your fears for your missing friends, the Toa Nuva, are blinding you to the real crisis on this island."

"That the Gukko birds of worry and care fly about your head, you cannot change," Velika chimed in. "But that they build nests in your mask, you can prevent."

"You're worried about six Toa," Garan continued, trying to be heard over the impacts of the blasts. "I have the whole Matoran population of this island to protect!"

"And you've been doing a real happy-cheer job of that, from what I've heard!" snapped Kongu. "First, we find the Toa Nuva. Then, we rescue the rest of your Matoran. Got it?"

"I thought Toa always put the interests of Matoran first," Garan said.

"I thought Matoran were taller," Kongu replied. "Just another of life's little disappointments. Listen, I understand you want to help your friends. But without the Toa Nuva, none of my friends would be alive. I owe them."

Nuparu shot by overhead, just barely avoiding the blasts of a second nektann. "You two want to stop arguing, and find a way to shut these things down?"

"You're the Toa of Earth!" Kongu shouted back. "Throw dirt at them or something!"

"The bird soars through the sky," Velika muttered. "But if I were a colossus, and the sky was beneath my feet, could it truly be said the bird flew underground?"

Before Kongu could ask just what the

Po-Matoran was talking about, Garan was yelling at Nuparu. "Down! Go down!" the Matoran said.

Nuparu obligingly went into a dive, firing his blaster drill as he went. The power of the weapon bore a hole in the ground beneath him. The nektann tried in vain to target the flying Toa, but couldn't compensate for his speed. An instant later, he had vanished underground.

"What just happened?" asked Kongu.

"Velika looks at things from a unique angle," said Garan. "He was suggesting a flying Toa of Earth might be well served by doing the same thing."

An explosion rocked the area, followed by another. Kongu peered over the boulder to see flames shooting up from both of the devastated nektann as the acrid smell of burning metal filled the air. The cause, a smiling Nuparu, emerged from the smoking wreckage a moment later.

"Armored all over," he said, "except at the bottom. One shot from below, and boom. I should have figured that out myself."

Velika smiled proudly and patted Toa Nuparu on the arm. For a moment, they weren't a Toa and a Matoran, but simply two inventors sharing a moment of accomplishment.

"We may want to save the congratulations for later," said Garan, pointing at the still-smoking wreckage. Some of the scattered pieces were beginning to move toward one another, as if drawn magnetically. Nuparu suddenly remembered tales of the Metru Nui Vahki reassembling themselves after defeats.

"Let's get inside before they finish," he said. "Round two might not go as smoothly."

The two Toa and two Matoran sprinted for the gateway. The workers who had crafted the door had made it well, with inches-thick stone and solid locks. Nuparu took aim with his blaster drill. Kongu reached out and gently lowered the Toa of Earth's weapon. "Too noisy. Let me," he said.

The Toa of Air unlimbered his crossbow in one smooth motion and fired. A bolt of energy pierced the lock as if it weren't there. The massive door swung open. Velika immediately began examining Kongu's weapon, muttering to himself in wonderment. Garan finally had to pull the diminutive tinkerer away.

Despite the warmth of the outside air, the interior of the stronghold was deathly cold. The party moved silently through the dark corridors, alert for any sound or movement. Kongu used his crossbow on every locked door they came across, hoping each time to find the Toa Nuva behind one of them. Instead, they found empty rooms, chambers filled with scraps of equipment, and one whose walls were covered with crude carvings reading "Vezok" and "Vezon."

"That makes no sense," Toa Nuparu whispered. "Vezok's a Piraka ... but *Vezon* is the Matoran word for 'double.' I don't see the connection."

By reflex, everyone turned to look at Velika. But the Po-Matoran just shrugged his shoulders.

The group inspected another score of empty chambers before finally reaching one that looked like it had been used recently. Huge, and packed from floor to ceiling with items both familiar and bizarre, it appeared to be a combination trophy room/training room. In one corner, a cage hung from the ceiling. In another was a stack of artifacts of unknown value, probably plundered from other islands during the Pirakas' past exploits. Two mechanisms occupied the center of the room, apparently designed to teach the user how to stay atop a wild animal. Their purpose was partially explained when Kongu found a carving that showed the Piraka riding what looked like the massive Tahtorak of Turaga Vakama's tales.

"Glad I missed that," the Toa of Air muttered.

"Kongu!" Toa Nuparu cried out. "Over here!"

Garan and Velika were already standing beside the Toa of Earth, looking up at the wall. The long shadows made it impossible for Kongu to see what they were reacting to until he got up close. Then he wished he had never looked.

Hanging from large, rusted nails were the

masks of the six Toa Nuva. Their reason for being on display was unmistakable: they were trophies of conquest.

"Mata Nui, preserve us," Nuparu whispered.

"It may already be too late for that," Kongu replied, shock in his voice. "I don't know what this means — whether they were simply brought to down-ground, or they're dead — but I do know they have to be avenged."

"Do we . . . do we take them with us?"

Kongu shook his head. "We have no way to easy-carry them and no suva to leave them on. We need our hands free for combat, Nuparu, especially now. They will be ever-safe here. Trust me, the Piraka won't get the chance to touch these masks again."

The two Toa and two Matoran departed the chamber. Silence hung over them the way that Visorak webs once shrouded Metru Nui. All along, Nuparu and Kongu had nursed the hope that they simply had to find the Toa Nuva, and then all would be right. Now they were faced with the very real possibility that there were no longer any Toa Nuva to find.

They continued their exploration of the stronghold with more urgency now. If their heroes were gone, there were still villains to find and punish. But all they found were deserted rooms, until finally a sharp turn led them into a massive central chamber that housed a huge vat of greenish-black virus. Garan winced as he remembered the defeat of the Toa Nuva and the Matoran resistance in this very room, not so long ago.

"The substance in that vat is what the Piraka used to enslave my people," Garan said. "They must never be allowed to do such a thing to others. We must destroy the virus."

"And what a terrible waste that would be," hissed a voice behind them.

The Toa and Matoran whirled to see Zaktan and the other Piraka, as well as Brutaka, standing in the entryway.

"I might not be able to recreate it," Zaktan

continued. "And then I would lose the chance to make you and your Toa companions kneel before the Piraka. It would be a fitting final memory of Voya Nui."

"Final, huh?" said Kongu, crossbow at the ready. "If you're planning a quick-trip, we'll be glad to help you get going."

"When we leave this wretched rock, we will be stepping over your corpses," snarled Brutaka.

"And with the Mask of Life in hand," Hakann added. He exchanged quick glances with Avak, Reidak, and Thok, all of whom gave subtle nods in return.

"Now the only question is, how do we go about ending your miserable lives?" Zaktan asked, as the protodites that made up his body made a sickening hum. "We've killed Toa in so many ways over the centuries, and I hate to repeat myself."

Further discussion was cut off by a massive explosion that blew the west wall to rubble. Toa Kongu glanced up in time to see a huge burst of fire, accompanied by a mountainous ball of ice.

Power Play

The blast was so violent that the crystal vat would have tipped over and shattered had Brutaka not raced over in time to save it.

Four powerful figures walked out of the cloud of smoke and dust. Toa Jaller, Toa Hahli, Toa Hewkii, and Toa Matoro surveyed the scene with grim determination and barely contained rage.

"Two choices," Jaller said. "You can leave this island now, under your own power, or we can throw you off. Choose the first — get out, stay out, and go far from our sight — and you can lead long, if rotten, lives." The Toa of Fire smiled. "Choose the second, and there won't be enough of you left to feed a Makuta fish."

Toa Nuparu and Toa Kongu moved to stand beside their comrades. All six unlimbered their weapons and summoned their elemental powers in preparation for battle.

"I'll give you some time to consider surrendering. Oops, time's up," said the Toa of Fire. "Let's do what we came here for, friends. Let's take them down!"

SIX

To Dalu, it looked as if all the energies of chaos had been unleashed inside the central chamber of the stronghold.

Elemental blasts flew everywhere, countered by the lethal eyebeams of the Piraka. Mortal enemies grappled in the shadows, one side fighting for power and greed, the other for the fate of all existence. It seemed like the uncontrolled blaze of battle, but the Ga-Matoran knew better. Jaller and Hewkii had a plan, and they were putting it into action.

First priority was isolating Brutaka, and that was Toa Hewkii's job. Using his elemental power, Hewkii erected stone barriers around Brutaka. Each one was swiftly smashed by the powerful being, only to be replaced by another.

"I can do this all day," Hewkii shouted. "How about you?"

"Do you think you can stop me with pebbles?" Brutaka bellowed in reply. "I have uprooted mountains, Toa. I have ridden the tornado and filled the earthquake with fear. When you were still toiling at your mundane Matoran chores, I and others like me were holding your universe together. Do you really believe your puny powers can threaten a member of the Order of Mata Nui?"

The news shook Hewkii to his core. How could this monster, this potential slayer of Toa, be associated in any way with the Great Spirit Mata Nui? No, it had to be a lie. Brutaka was counting on Hewkii to be distracted and provide him with an opening to attack.

"I'm not falling for that," said the Toa of Stone. "Why don't you fall instead?"

Hewkii's powers ripped open the stone floor of the stronghold and the bedrock below. Taken by surprise, Brutaka fell into the crevice. Hewkii then pulled stone from the walls and ceiling, sending it cascading down on top of Brutaka and effectively sealing the gap.

"Eat rock," said the Toa of Stone.

*   *   *

Nuparu dodged a vicious thrust of Zaktan's tri-bladed weapon. "What was the point?" said the Toa of Earth.

"The point of what?" snarled the Piraka.

"All this destruction . . . enslaving the Matoran . . . all of it. Why put them to work draining the volcano, when you Piraka could have done it much faster on your own?"

Zaktan smiled. "We don't like to get our claws dirty."

"Then you're going to hate this," Nuparu said. He triggered his elemental power, drawing the soil from the cracks in the stronghold floor and forming it into a fist. It slammed Zaktan, but when the cloud of dirt settled to the ground, the emerald-armored Piraka stood unharmed.

"You fool," Zaktan spat. "My power allows me to disperse my substance, allowing each grain of earth to pass through without ever touching me. It's a shame you can't do the same, Toa — it might spare you some pain."

With that, the microscopic protodites that

made up Zaktan's body began to drift apart. Soon, only his head remained solid, the rest of him transformed into a sickly green swarm that headed for Nuparu.

"Tell me, Toa," Zaktan said softly. "How long do you think it will take for you to go insane once you are in my embrace?"

"Oh, I've been crazy for years," answered Nuparu, grinning. "Ask anybody. After all, who else would do this?"

Calling upon his Kanohi Mask of Flight, Nuparu rocketed into the air straight at Zaktan. Just before he hit the swarm, the Toa of Earth began to rotate in midair, whirling his body faster and faster until he was only a blur. He hit the swarm with the force of a cyclone, pulling the protodites along in his wake as he headed for the chamber ceiling.

"I'm really not very good at this flying stuff," Nuparu said. He cracked his body like a whip, forcing Zaktan to slam into a wall. "I'm pretty poor at landing, so maybe I should just let you drop."

Zaktan's answer was a burst of laser vision that scorched Nuparu's shoulder armor and damaged the muscle inside. Nuparu yelled in pain and accelerated, heading out the ruined wall and over the island. As he passed the coast, he began a power dive toward Voya Nui Bay.

"Tell me something, Piraka," he said. "How well do you swim?"

Toa Kongu was in a unique situation. He had to keep his mouth shut.

He had not gone more than two steps when Avak's power to create the perfect prison enclosed him in what looked like a giant zamor sphere. Kongu barely had time to gulp a mouthful of air before the sphere turned into a vacuum chamber. Now, no matter how much air Kongu created with his elemental power, the sphere absorbed it. Opening his mouth would mean instant death.

"I was hoping for a fire or ice Toa," said Avak. "Much easier to lock up. But you'll do.

Might as well take a deep breath of nothing and get it over with, Toa."

Toa Kongu calculated he had about four seconds to live. None of the other Toa were close enough to help, and the Matoran had already left on their special mission. Fortunately, thanks to the Matoran, the Toa Inika knew a great deal more about the Piraka than the Piraka knew about them.

And you picked on the wrong Toa, Kongu thought as he unleashed the power of his Mask of Telepathy. Making contact with Avak's mind, Kongu sent screaming thoughts into the Piraka. Avak winced as a cacophony of deafening noise overwhelmed his mind. He staggered, dropped to his knees, and Kongu's prison evaporated along with his concentration.

Kongu gasped for breath. Then he walked over to Avak, grabbed the Piraka by the throat, and hauled him to his feet. "You tried too little air. Let's try too much."

So saying, Kongu's elemental power

reached out to encircle Avak. Slowly at first, then more rapidly, the air pressure increased around the startled Piraka. It quickly soared past the point where the internal pressure of Avak's body could compensate. Just shy of it becoming too much to bear, Kongu cut off the effect and Avak collapsed.

"You're right, next time maybe you should stick to a fire or ice Toa-hero," the Toa of Air said. "A lot less pressure."

Hakann looked around the chamber with increasing worry. Avak and Zaktan were down or gone, and the other Piraka were at best deadlocked with their opponents. Worse, Brutaka had not yet emerged from his makeshift tomb, and if he didn't, the special zamor sphere Hakann was carrying would go to waste.

It hadn't been easy to craft, but he had managed to create a sphere that carried a little bit of Vezok's power. It should have been just enough to accomplish what Hakann needed it to, if he could just find his target. Of course, he

had no intention of sharing the reward with anyone else.

There's only room for one supreme entity on this island, he told himself. *And I'm just made for that job.*

Toa Jaller spotted Hakann in the shadows, no doubt planning an escape. He couldn't allow that to happen. The Piraka had to be defeated right here and now and then be made to tell what had happened to the Toa Nuva. Hewkii had joined him to battle Reidak, when Jaller signaled that he was going after Hakann.

"Drop your weapons!" the Toa of Fire shouted at the crimson-armored Piraka. "Don't make me hurt you."

"Make you?" Hakann laughed. "Who could stop you? Admit it, Toa, you'd like nothing better than to burn this grin right off my face. You want to be standing on top of our corpses as the conquering hero. Strip off that mask and that high and mighty attitude, and you're no better than we are."

Jaller felt the heat rising in him. His flame wanted to leap out of his sword and make Hakann pay for his crimes, but Jaller kept it under control. "I'm nothing like you. We're fighting for the safety of this universe and the Matoran in it. What are you fighting for?"

Hakann slowly circled Jaller until he was facing the site where Brutaka was buried. "Yes, Toa always fight for the little Matoran, don't they? And when you win, they all cheer you and shout your name and build statues in your honor. You say you do it for right or justice, but you really do it for the hero worship. And that's the difference between us, Toa — I don't care what the Matoran think. I don't care what the Great Spirit Mata Nui thinks. I don't care what *anyone* thinks, and that's why I'll always be free and you'll always be fighting someone else's fights."

The Piraka's words caused Jaller to hesitate. Much as he hated to admit it, Hakann was uncomfortably close to the truth. After all, even before the Toa came to the island of Mata Nui, Jaller and his fellow Matoran had built statues of them and told and retold legends about them. Once they arrived, the Matoran treated them as heroes, maybe even as more than that. They were seen as infallible powerhouses who never knew doubt or fear and could never lose a battle. Even Tahu and the others started to see themselves that way, which was probably not a good thing.

Is it all about being cheered? Jaller wondered. *Are some of us thinking more about the reception we'll get on Metru Nui if we come back victors, when we should be focusing on the mission?*

"Somewhere, there are Toa fighting and dying right now, and when they're gone, no one will even remember their names," Hakann continued. "How many Matoran do you think recall the names of the Toa who fought in the war against the Dark Hunters? But they remember Makuta and Nidhiki and Roodaka. Good gets forgotten, evil never does."

"What's your point?" said Jaller.

"I'm giving you a chance," said Hakann. "You can keep on fighting us, and maybe even win . . . and then do it over again next month or next year, against some other foe . . . and on and on, until you're too old and tired to fight, and some Rahi turns you into scrap. That can be your life. Or you can join with us and be part of a legend Matoran will be repeating through all the many dark nights to come."

When Jaller replied, it was in a voice heavy with disgust. "I'm going to do the universe a favor, Piraka. I'm going to shut your mouth for good."

Hakann's eyes darted to the left. He could see the pile of rubble shifting as Brutaka dug his way out. An instant later, the head and shoulders of that mighty being forced their way through the jagged shards of stone. He would be free in a moment. The time to strike was now.

"Too bad, Toa. The offer to join us was only good for a limited time — and your time just ran out," the Piraka said.

It was then Jaller realized Hakann was taking aim with his zamor sphere launcher, not at him or the other Toa, but at Brutaka. Loaded in the weapon was a golden sphere which glowed with an unhealthy light. Something clicked in his mind and he suddenly knew what Hakann was about to do.

"No!" shouted Jaller, racing forward.

Nearby, Thok heard Toa Jaller's shout, saw Hakann taking aim, and knew he had to move. He lashed out and connected with Matoro, sending the Toa of Ice to the ground. Then he ran full speed for Hakann, diving at the last moment, his hands reaching out for the scarlet Piraka's armor. . . .

It happened so fast. It happened so slowly. Amazingly, both statements were true.

Hakann fired the zamor sphere, even as Thok collided with him and Jaller tried in vain to intervene. Brutaka never saw the sphere coming his way. It struck him in the side, dematerialized, and passed inside him. A second later, Brutaka's knees buckled as if he had been struck from behind. A bolt of black lightning flashed from Brutaka, striking Hakann, the energy surging through his body and Thok's.

Hakann roared. Thok staggered, fell back, and clutched the wall for support. Brutaka sagged and hit the floor, looking like he was dead.

Toa Jaller stopped short. Hakann was glowing with raw power. Grinning, the Piraka lightly tapped the Toa of Fire and sent Jaller flying across the length of the room. He struck the stone wall and his world went dark.

"I did it!" Hakann shouted. All over the chamber, Piraka and Toa stopped their battles to see what was happening. Thok had recovered his balance and now stood beside the red Piraka.

"We did it," said Thok, glaring at Hakann. "You tried to steal all the power for yourself. If I hadn't spotted you —"

"But you did," Hakann said. "And now we have the power to take whatever we want from this island. Then we'll destroy the Toa, the Dark Hunters, yes, even the Brotherhood of Makuta itself!"

Thok could feel how much his natural energies had grown. Using only the barest fraction of his new power, he brought the Piraka stronghold to life. Walls grew arms that reached out and seized the Toa and Piraka. The floor formed stone shackles to bind their legs. The building itself seemed to be laughing as it tightened its grip on its prisoners.

A second application of energy and a great stone hand rose from the floor, lifting Hakann and Thok into the air. From his high perch, Hakann looked down on the field of battle and smiled.

"The old has given way to the new," he proclaimed. "With the power of Brutaka now ours, we are the new masters of this universe. Now all that remains is to find the Mask of Life!"

"Traitor!" snarled Avak. "Do you think we'll let you two get away with this? Do you think we won't find a way to take revenge, even if we have to track you to the very edge of reality?"

"The Toa stand against you as well, Hakann," Toa Hahli shouted. "As long as we live, you will never have the mask!"

Hakann shrugged. Casually, as if swatting an insect, he unleashed a mental blast that ripped through the minds of all those below. Toa and Piraka alike screamed as the very act of thinking became an unbearable agony.

"Then live no longer," said the crimson Piraka.

SEVEN

Garan and his Matoran comrades moved carefully through the darkened corridors of the Piraka stronghold. The Toa Inika would surely keep the Piraka occupied, but there was always the chance that automated nektann might be positioned at key points. Garan kept his weapons ready, just in case.

Their mission was a vital one: Find the Toa Nuva, lead them back to their masks, and get them to join the fight. Of the Toa, only Matoro had the power to do a faster search, but in his wraith form the Toa Nuva would be unable to see or hear him. Garan had no doubt that part of Jaller's goal was to get the Matoran out of harm's way, but he also knew that the presence of the Toa Nuva could prove to be a crucial edge in the fight.

"I don't like this," said Dalu. "We should be back there fighting for our people."

"There were once two little lava rats who wished to cross a great chasm," replied Velika. "All day and all night, one carried small sticks and pebbles to the hole and dropped them in. He hoped that someday the hole would be filled. His brother rat, being the wiser, wandered the barrens until he found a Kikanalo. Sympathizing with the plight of the rats, the Kikanalo used his great strength to knock down a tree, making a bridge over the chasm across which the rats could travel."

"Um, yeah," said Piruk. "What he said."

"Good old Velika," commented Kazi. "Never use two words when 127 will do."

"Quiet," snapped Garan. "I found something."

He pushed open a thick iron doorway. The creak of the hinges sounded like thunder in the quiet corridor. There were no Toa Nuva inside, only scattered tablets. One in particular caught Garan's eye. It featured a map of Voya Nui, but not the island as it was now, rather as it had been a thousand years ago. Originally, Voya Nui had been more oval in shape, with a large, thriving village where the bay now existed. Centuries ago, the land on which that village rested had broken off and sunk into the sea, taking the village and its Matoran down to the bottom.

"These are histories," the Onu-Matoran said. "But much more recent than the ones we had. The Piraka must have brought these with them."

"How?" asked Balta. "How would they know anything about Voya Nui?"

"Someone had to be watching this place . . . or knew someone who had been," Garan answered. "They have the entire record of the sinking, and . . . ," His voice trailed off.

"What is it?" asked Dalu.

"This carving . . . it makes no sense," Garan said. "According to this, the village still exists! It's beneath the waves, but somehow our brother and sister Matoran have survived."

"Then why haven't they returned?" asked Balta. "Why haven't they sent some sign?"

"I don't know," Garan answered. "But when this island is free of Piraka, you can be sure we are going to find out."

Nuparu stepped through the gaping hole that once was a chamber wall. He carried an earthen cocoon on his shoulders, containing the semi-conscious form of Zaktan. The shock of hitting the water had knocked the Piraka leader out, but picking up and carrying a mass of billions of pro-todites had proved to be a problem. So Nuparu had simply encased him in earth, making sure it was porous enough to allow Zaktan to breathe.

He expected the battle to be over, one way or the other. But he wasn't prepared for the sight of a half-dead Brutaka and imprisoned Toa and Piraka. Dumping the cocoon on the floor, he ran and freed Jaller.

"What happened?"

"That's not as important as what's about to," Jaller answered. He strode over to where Brutaka lay and snapped, "You told them, didn't you?"

Brutaka said nothing.

"You know the location of the Mask of Life. After Hakann and Thok stole your power, they gave you a choice, didn't they? Tell them where the mask is, or die."

"Jaller, that makes no sense," said Hahli. "He would have been unconscious from Hakann's mental blast, just like the rest of us."

"Would he? Kongu, use your mask and read his mind."

Toa Kongu triggered the power of the Mask of Telepathy and tried to scan Brutaka's thoughts. After a few moments, he shook his head and gave up. "His mind is shielded."

"Exactly. From what Hewkii and Balta have told me, it's clear that Axonn and Brutaka were on the island to protect the mask. With that sort of valuable secret in their heads, it only makes sense they would be shielded against telepathy or mental attack. Nothing could make them part with that knowledge — except cowardice."

"Or necessity." The words came from Axonn, who stood amidst the rubble of the wall.

Toa Jaller turned to face the newcomer. "Who are you? What are you?"

"It's enough that you can be sure we are on the same side, Toa," said Axonn. "And I think who I am is less important than what I know."

"Hakann and Thok are on their way to get the mask," said Jaller. "We need to know where it is so we can stop them."

"I'll stop them," Axonn said, turning away.

Jaller stunned everyone in the chamber by grabbing Axonn roughly and pulling him back. "We don't have time for this! I don't care how powerful you are, we can't let the safety of the universe depend solely on one being. For good or ill, we're Toa, Axonn — tell us where the enemy has gone and let us do our jobs."

Axonn looked from his former friend, Brutaka, to the Toa. He hated to admit it, but Jaller was right. The stakes were too high for pride to dictate his decisions. "Come with me, out of the Piraka's hearing, and I will tell you all I know."

"Hold it!" shouted Avak, still bound by Thok's creation. "You need us!"

"Right," said Kongu. "Like we need a second shadow plague."

"Maybe you won't talk so much, Toa, with your mask stuffed in your mouth," growled Reidak.

"You know and we know: The only way you are going to stop Hakann and Thok is to reverse what they did to Brutaka," Avak continued. "And only we know how to do that. We'll make a zamor sphere that can reverse the process, but only if we go with you."

Hewkii smiled. "We could find other ways to get the information from you."

Avak laughed. "Even if you had the will — and you don't, Toa, not 'heroes' like you — you don't have the time."

"He's right," said Hahli. "We don't. And, Hewkii, we can't afford to become worse than the enemies we fight."

An unpleasant decision was finally reached.

The four Piraka were freed, on condition they create a zamor sphere that could undo what had been done to Brutaka. While they did that, Axonn examined the empty spheres that already existed, as if they were the most fascinating things he had ever seen.

Toa Kongu, on the other hand, was drawn to the vat containing the virus used to enslave the Matoran. There was something about the eddies and currents in the substance, and how it moved inside the crystal. A Ga-Matoran would have called it an "angry sea."

He reached out an armored hand and touched the glass. Without his conscious urging, the Mask of Telepathy activated, sending tendrils of thought into the vat. Kongu leapt back suddenly as if jolted by an electric shock.

Kongu stood, frozen, and just stared at the vat for several minutes. It took him that long to even allow himself to consider what he had just experienced through the power of the mask.

Whatever is inside that crystal . . . inside the

zamor spheres the Piraka used . . . it's alive, he realized.

Alive . . . and evil.

Axonn handed Toa Jaller a strangely glowing zamor sphere. "You're going to need this."

"For what?"

"Jaller, the Mask of Life is not just any Kanohi. It's powerful . . . in the wrong hands, devastating . . . and it needs protection," Axonn replied. "Ages ago, at almost the dawn of time, my people hid the mask away and placed guardians around it."

"You and Brutaka," Jaller said, nodding.

Axonn smiled sadly. "Oh, if it were only us there might be no danger. No, what protects the Mask of Life are things infinitely worse — beings beyond good or evil, who exist for one purpose: to keep the unworthy away from the mask. Even I, one of those assigned to protect this ultimate Kanohi, would not be allowed to lay hands upon it without first overcoming them."

"So if we defeat them — if we prove our-selves worthy — we can get the Mask of Life," Jaller said. "And if we're unworthy?"

"They will kill you," Axonn answered.

Jaller glanced to the right and saw Zaktan handing over a zamor sphere to Toa Hewkii. In theory, this sphere would reverse Hakann's actions and return the stolen power to Brutaka. *Then we'll just have six treacherous Piraka to deal with,* he thought.

"It looks like we're ready to get moving," said the Toa of Fire. "Are you coming with us?"

"No," Axonn replied. "I'm staying here."

"I see. As backup, just in case we fail?"

Axonn shook his head and looked at Brutaka, still semiconscious on the floor. "No, Toa. Just in case you succeed."

EIGHT

I should have done this centuries ago, thought Hakann happily. *What power! I can't imagine why, with this sort of energy coursing inside him, Brutaka would have chosen to stay on this miserable spit of land.*

A small, climbing Rahi scurried through the trees above. With a casual thought, Hakann struck the creature with a mental blast and fried its mind. It tumbled from the trees and fell dead at the Piraka's feet.

Life is good, Hakann said to himself. *But for some beings, the alternative is better.*

Behind him, Thok's thoughts were not quite so cheerful. True, he was enjoying the increased power and even toyed with the idea of bringing a mountain to life just to see what that would be like. But he also knew he could not turn his back on Hakann for even a moment. His "ally" would gladly strike him down or somehow steal all the power for himself, given half a chance.

So maybe I should do it first. He considered the idea. It was true that he might need Hakann's help to get the Mask of Life, but once they had it, one of them would have to go, anyway. *If that's the case, it might as well be Hakann, and it might as well be now,* Thok decided.

The timing was perfect. Hakann had his back turned and was absorbed in his own thoughts. All Thok had to do was bring a slab of rock to life and —

Hakann's lava launcher suddenly flipped backward on his arm and fired. A massive ball of magma struck Thok dead-on, sending him hurtling through the trees. The strange forest caught on fire, flames eating away at centuries-old trees. A stunned Thok could see Hakann approaching through the smoke and flames.

"Thok, you poor, pathetic excuse for a schemer," said Hakann. "You couldn't defeat me when I was merely a Dark Hunter. You didn't even have the courage to try when I was a Piraka. And now you think you can strike me down, when so much power is at my command?"

Thok didn't waste energy replying. Instead, he let his power flow out of him and into the trees, the rocks — even the flames themselves. All of these things became his to command, and all directed their fury at Hakann. Taken by surprise, the crimson-armored Piraka was forced back, giving Thok time to rise to his feet and get away from the blaze.

"This island is mine to use," Thok shouted. "All of it! And if I keep battering you with wood, rock, and fire, you won't be able to concentrate enough to use your mental blasts, Hakann. Think about it — here you are, almost within reach of the Mask of Life, but you'll never live to see it."

There was truth in Thok's words, though Hakann refused to accept it. Desperately, he lashed out with mind blasts at the animated creatures attacking him. But the beings of wood and rock and flame had no minds to blast. They existed only because Thok had willed them to exist.

Willed them . . . and controls them, Hakann thought. *And he can't control what he can't see.*

Aiming his lava launcher at the ground, Hakann hurled three giant bursts of magma. When they hit, the result was a firestorm that turned the forest to ash and effectively blocked Hakann off from Thok's sight. Instantly, the attacks on Hakann ceased, and Thok's creations went back to being inanimate.

Now the two Piraka both went into motion, each trying to spot the other through the flames. Neither shouted any boasts or threats. There was no point in giving one's position away by talking.

Then Thok caught a break. He spotted Hakann maneuvering toward a better position on some high ground. From there, he would have a clear shot with his zamor sphere launcher and Thok would end up no better than a slave.

Thok tracked Hakann carefully, and at the right moment, his eyebeams lanced out at his foe. Instantly, Hakann's world began to spin crazily around as Thok's spellbinder vision robbed him of his sense of balance. He couldn't use any of his weapons or abilities, since he had no way to aim them. Just trying to take a step forward resulted in Hakann's falling face down on the ground.

Thok laughed at the sight. Striding up to the fallen Piraka, he said, "That's where you belong, groveling in the dirt. Who knows? Maybe a few more blasts and the effect will be permanent."

Hakann growled in frustration. To have Thok so close and not be able to do anything. Mental blasts, lava launcher, heat vision, all useless, all —

Hakann stopped. He smiled — not easy to do when your face is in the dirt. There was a chance, maybe a slim one, and if his plan worked, he would probably wind up dead. *But with any luck, Thok will go first,* Hakann thought.

Hakann unleashed the power of his heat vision. He fired twin blasts into the earth, willing them to penetrate through soil and rock. In his mind's eye, he pictured the searing beams of heat melting everything in their path until they reached the target he hoped was down below.

Then the time for hoping and wishing was over, as a cataclysmic explosion tore the ground to pieces and sent both Piraka hurtling into the air. Of the two, only Hakann was smiling about it.

Toa Jaller saw the flames in the distance, followed by the huge explosion. "Well, at least they aren't making it hard to track them."

Nuparu took off into the sky and zoomed over the devastated area. He couldn't see either of the Piraka in all the smoke and dust, but he knew the two of them being disintegrated was too much to hope for. He turned back and landed beside Jaller and Hahli.

"I'm surprised that didn't happen before," said the Toa of Earth. "A Piraka with heat vision on a volcanic island probably riddled with gas pockets. One glance in the wrong direction and *boom*."

Toa Kongu ran toward them. "They're both alive, but thought-jumbled. We need to strike now!"

Jaller turned to the others. "We move in.

Kongu, you're with Nuparu; Hahli, with Hewkii; Matoro, with me; and the Piraka —"

"Will see to themselves," Zaktan finished harshly. "We agreed to help you for our own reasons. We did not agree to take your orders, Toa."

"Maybe you'd rather go for another swim?" asked Nuparu, smiling.

Zaktan's answer was a snarl and a glare of pure hatred. Then he and the other Piraka left the path, vanishing among the rocks.

"Should we just let them go?" asked Hahli.

"They may be taking a different route, but they're headed the same place we are," answered Jaller. "Straight into the fire."

Even with Brutaka's power added to his own, Hakann hurt. Not surprising, considering the explosion had vaporized a huge chunk of forest and sent up a fireball that could be seen all over the island. It was amazing that he had survived, and it would be a miracle if Thok had done the same. *Good thing Piraka don't believe in miracles,* he thought.

In addition to probably killing Thok, the explosion had produced one other happy circumstance: It had blown away the false rock wall that concealed the entrance to a long and winding staircase that led beneath the island. He remembered Brutaka's words, then.

"A stairway . . . ancient and seemingly unending," Brutaka had said, as the two Piraka hovered over him. "It leads down, down below the volcano and its lake of lava, all the way to the Chamber of the Mask. But you won't make it that far . . . the guardians of the Mask of Life will grind you into atoms and scatter you in the magma."

Hakann's recollection stopped there. He took a few steps toward the opening and then stopped. "You know, it is almost a shame I left the other Piraka behind," he said to himself. "Zaktan and the rest could have gone first — that way, if there was atom-grinding to be done, it would have happened to them."

"Always thinking of others, aren't you?" said Zaktan.

Hakann whirled to see the four Piraka assembled before him, weapons at the ready. They looked so fierce, yet their power was so insignificant next to his, that he found it hard not to laugh.

"I wondered when you would show up," he said. "I hope you stopped to kill those annoying Toa before you left the stronghold. Masks and morality are such a boring combination."

Avak struck first. Using his power to create a living prison, he brought a cage of ice into being around Hakann. He then gave the bars a solid whack, causing them to vibrate and give off a loud hum. The sonics were meant to distract the captive and keep him from using his mental blasts.

"Very . . . effective," Hakann said slowly. "There's only . . . one problem with a cage . . . designed to hold Hakann. . . ."

The crimson Piraka lashed out with his fist and smashed the ice bars to pieces.

"It wouldn't hold Brutaka," he finished.

Zaktan hurled part of his substance at Hakann, the buzzing protodites making right for his foe's smiling face. Hakann responded by using his enhanced powers to raise the body temperature of the first thousand or so by several hundred degrees. One by one, they combusted, vanishing in puffs of smoke.

"I love the smell of burning protodite," Hakann growled. "Don't you?"

The powerful Piraka took a few steps forward, raising his lava launcher. "Now why don't I be a merciful being and finish you off?"

The ball of magma appeared in the weapon, ready to shoot out and eliminate Hakannn's former teammates. Then a thick coating of ice suddenly appeared around the launcher, heavy enough to throw Hakann off balance. Reidak didn't stop to ask how that was possible. He simply launched himself at Hakann, slamming into him and sending him stumbling backward.

Vezok turned to see Thok approaching, wisps of frost still coming from his ice weapon. "Thanks for the save," Vezok said.

"Don't be silly," Thok replied. His weapon

fired again, freezing Vezok solid. "I'm not on your side."

A blast of fire cut across Thok's path. Toa Jaller stood on a rocky outcropping, looking down upon him. "Then maybe it's time you were on no side at all, Piraka," Jaller said.

"You wish," snarled Thok, raising his ice weapon. Before he could fire it, energy bolts began raining down on him from the air. He looked up to see Toa Nuparu in flight, carrying Toa Kongu and his energy crossbow.

Thok didn't give up easily. He hurled a bolt of ice at Jaller and Matoro, but the two Toa Inika were ready for him. They matched his blast with ones of their own — lightning mixed with fire and frost.

"Great thing about ice," Toa Nuparu shouted down from above. "It's just frozen water."

Jaller and Matoro's blasts struck Thok's ice bolt. The Piraka's powers checked theirs, but the lightning that was interlaced with the Toa's energy could not be stopped.

"And water is a great conductor of electricity," Nuparu continued.

The lightning bolts traveled up the ice and back to Thok, blowing him off his feet. He flew 50 feet and slammed into a hillside.

"Or did you already know that?" added Nuparu.

On the other side of the battle, Hakann had succeeded in tearing Reidak off him. "Last time, you threw *me* into a battle," said the crimson Piraka. "Now *I'll* return the favor."

With blinding speed, Hakann hurled Reidak at the other Piraka. Avak couldn't dodge in time and took the impact full on. Zaktan saw what was coming and managed to shift his protodite substance out of the way.

"The Toa will take care of Thok," Zaktan hissed. "But you're mine."

Zaktan fired his laser vision. Hakann responded with his heat vision. Halfway between the two, the beams impacted each other. The resulting burst of energy staggered and blinded both. Hakann's sight recovered first and he lunged for Zaktan.

Or, rather, he tried to — a pair of strong hands erupted from underground, grabbing his ankles. "That's not very sporting," said Toa Hewkii, head popping up from the soil. "If you're not going to play by the rules, you'll have to be penalized!"

Hewkii gave an enormous shove and let go, sending Hakann hurtling into the air. The Piraka wheeled in midflight to fire his heat beams, only to be met by a blast of water laced with lightning.

Thok was back on his feet. Although he knew the Toa and Piraka were the immediate problem, he couldn't waste the chance to strike at Hakann. Using his power, he froze Toa Hahli's column of water, trapping Hakann in a tower of ice. Then Thok marched forward, casually smashing the tower with a sweep of his fist as he went by. A few seconds later, he heard Hakann slam into the ground behind him.

Toa Nuparu spotted Thok on the move and tried to warn Kongu, but it was too late. Thok's spellbinder vision struck the Toa of Earth, destroying his ability to see straight. His flight out of control, he plunged toward the ground.

"This is why miners shouldn't drive," Kongu grumbled as he called on his elemental power of air. There wasn't enough time to create an updraft that would keep them afloat. The best he could do was a cushion of air so that their impact wouldn't leave them a pile of shattered armor. An instant later, they hit hard.

"That's two down," said Thok. "Maybe I should bring the earth and rocks to life and bury them, Toa. What do you think?"

"Who says you'll get the chance?" Toa Jaller answered.

Beside Jaller, Matoro suddenly collapsed. Thok laughed, saying, "Toa fainting from fear — this is a day that will live in legend!"

Not for the reason you think, Matoro said to himself as his spirit raced across the battlefield.

He was counting on Hahli's ability to see and talk with him even in this form. He spotted her and, more importantly, she spotted him. As quickly as he could, he told her his plan.

"I would call this a stalemate," said Thok. "You Toa back off — all the way off Voya Nui — or your two friends become permanent parts of the island. And you know I'll do it."

"Of course you would," Jaller replied. "You're a Piraka. In place of honor, you have greed; in place of duty, you have treachery; and in place of a heart, you have an empty black pit. Even the Mask of Life couldn't change the fact that you're dead inside, Thok, and always will be."

"Words," spat Thok. "You Toa are always so good with words, when it's actions that matter."

"Then how's this?" asked Hahli. Triggering her elemental power, she turned the ground beneath Thok into a swamp. The Piraka sank like a rock up to his neck.

"Go ahead and freeze it," Hahli continued. "Or can't you break out of your own ice?"

Thok struggled to find his footing in the soft mud. There was no way to get any leverage to push himself out. That left freezing, then shattering the swamp, if the power stolen from Brutaka was up to doing that. He couldn't be sure.

The next moment, someone had seized Thok by the spine and hauled him out of the mud. It was a battered and bruised Hakann, armor chipped and cracked, who looked at Thok with undisguised contempt.

"Here I give you the chance to go down in history as the being who defeated six Toa, and what do you do?" Hakann said. "You fall in a mud puddle. Pathetic."

"Says the being who looks like he's been playing tag with a Kikanalo herd," Thok answered.

"We both have half of Brutaka's power," Hakann said. "If we want to devastate these Toa, we have to work together, as much as it disgusts me to admit it."

"Side-by-side, hitting with all our powers at once," agreed Thok.

The two Piraka turned to face Jaller, Hahli, Hewkii, and the now-revived Matoro. Strangely, Zaktan was nowhere to be seen, but they knew they could deal with him later. Summoning all of their own energies and those they had stolen from Brutaka, they readied the one blow that would destroy all of their enemies.

It was the moment Toa Hewkii had been waiting for. Even as the Piraka's blasts sped toward him and the others, he launched the special zamor sphere Zaktan had created. It struck Thok and Hakann in the one tiny spot where each of their armor had made contact.

The Piraka's energies struck home, scattering the four Toa like dry leaves in a cyclone. At the same time, the zamor sphere hit, ripping away the stolen power in a flash of black lightning and sending it speeding back to its rightful owner. Shocked by the sudden loss of power, both Piraka sank to the ground and passed out.

Thus, there was no one still conscious on

the battlefield to see Zaktan's protodites slowly drift together above the bodies of Hakann and Thok. And there was no one to hear the Piraka leader say, "Now, my treacherous companions, my hunters in the dark . . . now the true battle begins."

NINE

Axonn started at the sight of Brutaka's eyes flashing back to life. The Toa and Piraka had succeeded, then, at defeating Thok and Hakann, and taking back the power they had stolen. But whether that could be called a "victory" was debatable, for it left Brutaka restored to his full might.

"You were hoping I would die," Brutaka said, rising. "That way, your conscience would be clear."

"I think that was *your* wish," Axonn replied. "An end to the miserable, empty existence you have made for yourself. But now you have a second chance, Brutaka."

"At what? Being a good little soldier for the Order of Mata Nui? Serving the will of some entity who's either dead or dying, depending on whom you talk to? Spending another thousand

115

or ten thousand or a hundred thousand years on this rock, guarding a mask instead of using it for my own benefit?"

"You know what the Mask of Life is meant to be used for," said Axonn. "And you know who is meant to use it — and it's not you. What would you do with it?"

Brutaka smiled. "We know what we were *told* the mask does. What if we were lied to? What if that mask makes its wearer as powerful as the Great Spirit Mata Nui? What if it gives you a universe to rule?"

"Then it would be a monstrous thing," Axonn replied. "For beings like you and I, even the Toa, could not be trusted with such power. Besides, you know I cannot be deceived. The legend of the Mask of Life is living truth . . . and you will not taint that mask with your touch."

Brutaka spun his twin-bladed sword rapidly, passing it from hand to hand faster than Axonn's eyes could follow. "Cannot be deceived? I guess I should be glad, then, that you can still be destroyed."

"My life doesn't matter," Axonn answered, mighty axe poised to defend himself. "Neither does yours. Only the mask matters, and if I have to fight you for eternity to protect it, then that is what I shall do."

"Then get ready, old friend," Brutaka said, eyes shrouded in darkness. "Eternity begins now."

Toa Hahli was the first to awaken. For a brief moment, she reflected on how glad she was the Toa Inika did not travel with a Chronicler. *No Matoran could have survived this,* she thought, looking around at the devastation. *Not even one with the luck of Takua.*

She checked on Nuparu and Kongu. Though hurt, they were both still alive, and a cooling mist revived them. The same applied to Jaller, Hewkii, and Matoro. Of the six, Jaller was in the best shape, his mask having somehow allowed him to dodge most of the blast.

"Where are the Piraka?" he asked, looking around.

"They were gone when I woke up," said

Hahli. "It's too much to hope that they found wisdom and fled the island, right?"

"We all know where they fled," Matoro answered. "Into yet another dark tunnel in a universe that seems to be filled with them. Next time we go on a hike, Jaller, remind me to bring some extra lightstones — maybe twenty thousand."

"We go after them," said Hewkii. It was a statement, not a question.

"Axonn? The Toa Nuva?" asked Kongu.

"No time," said Jaller. "Whether or not it was our destiny to find the Mask of Life when we got here, I think it's our destiny now. There's no one else to do it."

"Is that what heroes are, I wonder?" Hahli mused. "Beings who do what they have to do, because they have no other choice?"

"Turaga Nuju once speak-said that no one would ever choose to be a Toa," said Kongu. "No one except a crazy Le-Matoran, that is."

"Maybe you don't choose a destiny like that," Nuparu said softly. "Maybe it chooses you."

Together, the six Toa Inika turned toward

the entrance to the great stairway leading to the Mask of Life. They were ready to meet any dangers or enemies they might encounter on the way. They were ready to meet their destiny.

Far below, at the bottom of the 777 stairs that led to the Chamber of Life, there was a stirring in a river of lava. To anyone unfamiliar with the place, it might have seemed like a stray current in the molten magma. But for the flying Rahi who infested the ceiling of the chamber, it was a sight to freeze their blood.

A long leg emerged from the lava, its movements both amazingly graceful and thoroughly repulsive. It was followed by another and another, until a monstrous creature had emerged from the fiery liquid. Even more disturbing than the beast was the rider on its back, a masked being whose eyes glittered with madness.

"They're coming, Fenrakk," he whispered. "Can you feel them? So many coming to visit us. Do they want to visit, or do they just want the mask? What do you think?"

There was no answer, just the sound of lava dripping off the hair on the creature's legs and landing on the stone floor with a hiss.

"Yes, you're right," said the rider grimly. "They want the mask. But they can't have it, can they? Oh, no, it's mine . . . it's ours. Without it, what would we have to talk about? Our friendship is based on the mask, after all. Remember what it was like before? My trying to spear you, and your trying to devour me . . . not at all the way friends behave."

The Rahi up above had heard enough. They screeched and flew off up the staircase, eager to put distance between themselves and this strange pair. The rider's eyes narrowed, and he fired a burst of energy from his spear. It struck one of the Rahi, splitting the small flier into two smaller and weaker beings, each with only one wing. Both plunged to the ground and died on impact.

"Tsk, tsk," the rider said. "I really need to master this spear someday, even if I have to kill everything in sight to do it."

Beneath him, the creature called Fenrakk

tensed. The rider knew well this meant the beast had sensed the approach of enemies.

"What shall we do?" asked the rider. "Hide in the lava and spring upon them? Drop from the ceiling? So few make it down here, we must make the experience entertaining for them. After all, it is the last experience they will ever have."

The eyes of Fenrakk and its rider were riveted to the bottom of the staircase. Soon, newcomers would emerge through the doorway, provided none of the others up above killed them first. Then it would be time to welcome them properly.

"That's a good idea," whispered the rider. "We'll just stand very still and quiet. When they come, they won't even notice us. Or if they do, they'll think, 'Look how still and quiet they are. They would never harm an insect.' Yes, they will see how well we behave and not be afraid to come close and then . . . and then . . ."

Then it was time to wait. It might be days before the visitors came, or weeks, or they might never come at all. But in this darkened chamber ringed by lava, what else was there to do but long for the presence of another living being, the sound of another voice ... even if the being would not be living very long and the voice would sadly be stilled.

After all, thought Vezon, rider of the monstrous Fenrakk. *The waiting is half the fun.*